For Sông

MY
FOOTPRINTS

written by Bao Phi * Illustrated by Basia Tran

raintree
a Capstone company — publishers for children

Raintree is an imprint of Capstone Global Library Limited, a company incorporated in England and Wales having its registered office at 264 Banbury Road, Oxford, OX2 7DY – Registered company number: 6695582

www.raintree.co.uk
myorders@raintree.co.uk

Text © Bao Phi 2020

Edited by Kristen Mohn
Designed by Kay Fraser
Original illustrations © Capstone Global Library Limited 2020
Media research by Morgan Walters
Production by Laura Manthe
Printed and bound in India

ISBN 978 1 4747 6243 4

British Library Cataloguing in Publication Data
A full catalogue record for this book is available from the British Library.

Pronunciation help

Thuy (Twee)

Arti (AR-tee)

Ngoc (Ynyow)

Phoenix (FEE-nix)

Sarabha (sa-ra-BA)

Thuy sees those kids laughing at her again. She stomps away from school. The crisp, white blanket of new snow cracks like eggshells beneath her feet. She looks behind her and sees her jagged footprints.

"Footprints," she says. "My footprints!"

Thuy stops. She looks up at the branches that reach like
gloved fingers into the sky and sees a red bird.

"Where are your friends?" Thuy asks. "Don't you fly
south with the rest of the birds?"

The bird doesn't answer. *Maybe he doesn't feel like talking right now*, Thuy thinks. The little bird could fly away into the giant pane of sky if it felt in danger.

Thuy points her feet in a *V* shape and hops once, lightly, leaving shallow prints. She stops and draws a line through the middle of each *V* to make a third claw.

"Chirp chirp chirp!" Thuy squeaks and flaps her arms.

Almost home. The houses grow closer together. She can't read the
bubbly words of graffiti on the train carriages, but she thinks they are beautiful.

She remembers how she saw a deer here once, how out of place it
looked – but she knew its family must have been close.

"My footprints," Thuy whispers.

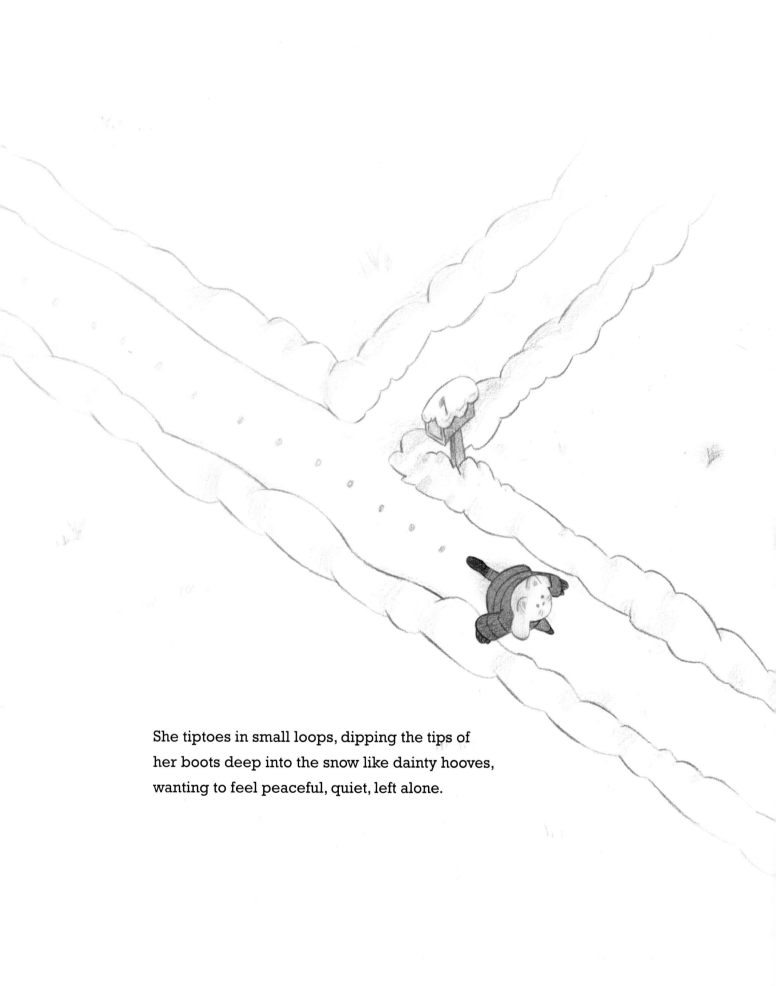

She tiptoes in small loops, dipping the tips of
her boots deep into the snow like dainty hooves,
wanting to feel peaceful, quiet, left alone.

Mummy Ngoc and Mummy Arti smile at Thuy when she gets home. Thuy knows they are both tired from work, but their smiles feel like a heater that warms Thuy's snow-wet toes.

"How was school, sweetie?" Mummy Ngoc asks.

Thuy doesn't want to answer that question. Instead she asks, "Do snakes have bottoms?"

"What?" Mummy Arti laughs.

Thuy laughs at first too, then frowns. She feels like a sudden snowstorm.

"Are you OK?" Mummy Ngoc asks.

"I don't want to talk about it!" Thuy shouts.

As she shuffles away, leaving tracks like a snake slithering through the snow, she hears her mothers talking. Mummy Arti's voice sounds frayed but warm, like Thuy's favourite blanket.

Thuy runs a stick along a fence that's missing two teeth like she is.

She makes more footprints, this time running faster so they are further apart. Quick, quick, quick!

"My footprints!" Thuy pants.

She is a spotted leopard that can blend into its surroundings and disappear if it's threatened.

"Meow!" Thuy screeches, though that doesn't seem quite right.

"My footprints," Thuy says, stomping deep into the snow.

She looks behind her and sees a grizzly bear's paw prints.
Strong and brave, a bear stands up for itself. Other animals
are afraid to make fun of it.

"RAWR!" Thuy growls, baring her teeth.

Mummy Arti and Mummy Ngoc come out into the tiny, snowy back garden polka-dotted by Thuy's footprints.

"What is the strongest animal?" Thuy asks.

Mummy Arti thinks, then says, "There are lots of different ways to be strong. An eagle is strong at flying in the sky. A dolphin is strong at swimming in the sea."

"And what do you think?" Mummy Ngoc asks Thuy.

"Maybe a dragon!" Thuy says. She imagines one with googly eyes and a long body and whiskers fluttering like a flag among the clouds. But she can't imagine its footprints.

"How about an elephant?" Mummy Arti suggests.

Thuy puts both her feet together like an elephant hoof and stomps one big hole in the deep snow. She wishes she could make four all at once.

"I want to be the biggest and strongest and scariest monster,"
Thuy says, "so that if kids at school make fun of me for having
two mums, or tell me to go back to where I come from, or call me
names, or bother me because I'm a girl, I can make them stop!"

"Can we play with you?" asks Mummy Ngoc.

"Yes," Thuy says. "Let's make footprints."

Mummy Ngoc says, "I wonder what creature we can pretend to be together, because we're stronger together."

"What's your favourite?" Thuy asks her.

"The phoenix!" Mummy Ngoc says.

Thuy sees their shadows curl into long blue feathers.

"Rise from the ashes!" she shouts, remembering a story about the powerful creature. The three of them hold hands with Thuy in the middle, then spread their arms wide so that together their shadows form a great wingspan.

"And what's your favourite, Mummy?" Thuy asks Mummy Arti.

"Do you remember the painting I showed you once, of the Sarabha?" Mummy Arti asks.

"Part lion, part bird!" Thuy says.

The three of them stand in a row, hands on hips, and they become the fearless, many-legged creature.

"An unexpected combination of beautiful things!" Thuy yells as their Sarabha marches through the snow.

"What's your favourite?" Mummy Arti asks Thuy.

"I want to make one up!" Thuy says. "It can fly and swim and run, and it is always kind to everyone else and only eats birthday cake."

"What does it look like?" Mummy Ngoc asks.

"It has black hair and black eyes, it's both a boy and a girl, and its skin keeps changing colour from black to light brown to lighter and back to black – not to hide, but because it always wants to be different shades of pretty – and it never hurts or makes fun of anyone."

"That sounds like my new favourite creature!" Mummy Arti says, her laughter a warm bubble. "What's its name?"

"Its name is Snakebottom!" Thuy says, then changes her mind.

"No, it's Arti-Thuy-Ngoc-osaurus!"

As the three of them hold hands, they make footprints together – the footprints of the rare and beautiful and strong and brave and quick and quiet Arti-Thuy-Ngoc-osaurus – in the fine, cold snow.

Thuy starts to chant, "Our footprints! Our footprints!"

PHOENIX

A phoenix or fenghuang is an immortal, bird-like creature from East Asian mythology meant to symbolize the masculine and feminine, and harmony and happiness. The phoenix from Greek mythology is a bird that rises from its own ashes in a rebirth. Mummy Ngoc's phoenix contains elements of both, as a symbol of the Eastern and Western influences in her life.

SARABHA

A Sarabha (or Sharabha) is a powerful, roaring creature from Hindu mythology that is sometimes described as a combination of a lion and a bird, or a many-legged deer. Mummy Arti chooses the brave and beautiful Sarabha to help give Thuy courage.

Author's note

As a bookish refugee growing up in an area and era where toughness was valued in boys, I am intimately familiar with bullying. Now that I'm a father, there is a long list of things I worry about for my daughter, and on that list is being erased or bullied because of her race, her gender presentation, her economic class or who she decides to love. One thing that may be universal to all parents is that we want our kids to have an easier, better life than we did. Perhaps one way to help advance a better world is to have these difficult conversations with our children rather than dismissing them or pretending they don't hurt. And I have a lot of my own work to do, because even though I survived an enormous amount of violence, discrimination and bullying, I know that I have at times also participated in systems of harm against other marginalized people. When have I been cruel when I could have been kind? When was I headstrong when I could have listened? I knew I wanted to write a book about bullying, but one that focused on the strength of love and community rather than revenge or dismissal. I wanted to write a book that challenged not only the mainstream community's perception of what is a family, but also my own.

While this story draws upon my own personal experience, I also needed to consult with those whose own identities and experiences more closely mirrored the people in the story. I am indebted to the following people, who read the manuscript and offered everything from advice to suggestions for names: Dr Sarah Park Dahlen, Que-Lam Huynh, Leah Lakshmi Piepzna-Samarasinha, Leilani ly-huong Nguyen, Molly Beth Griffin, Parag Khandhar, Juliana Hu Pegues, Raquel (Rocki) Simões and Luca Maria Raffo-Simões. Thanks also to the fine folks at Capstone, especially Kristen Mohn, for making the book better. And big thanks to Basia Tran, whose stunning art breathed a lovely life into this story.

More generally, I want to thank the families of the Twin Cities, especially Powderhorn, Minneapolis, for being a place where books like this are both welcomed and challenged. Last but not least, I would like to thank my daughter, Sông Phi-Hu, who upon making tracks in the Minnesota snow and chanting happily, "My footprints, my footprints!" gave me the idea of the hook for this book. With her permission, of course.

photo credit: Sông Phi-Hu

About the author

Bao Phi is an award-winning poet and children's book author. His stunning debut children's book with illustrator Thi Bui, *A Different Pond*, won a Caldecott Honor, a Charlotte Zolotow Award, an Asian/Pacific American Award for Literature, an Ezra Jack Keats Honor, a Boston Globe-Horn Book Honor, and numerous other awards and accolades. *My Footprints* is his second children's book. Bao is a single co-parent father, an arts administrator and a book nerd.

About the illustrator

Basia Tran is a Polish-Vietnamese illustrator working in books, music, animation, video games and advertising. Her diverse work and interests are all connected by a common thread: her desire to tell stories that can make people laugh, teach them something new or even bring them peace. In her free time, Basia is rock climbing, enjoying tea and thinking about all there is to learn and explore in the universe – often all at the same time. She currently lives in Kraków, Poland.